SPORT

Ship Dog of the Great Lakes

WRITTEN BY PAMELA CAMERON

ILLUSTRATED BY RENÉE GRAEF

Pamela Cameron
South Haven, Michigan
2022

With a storm rolling in over Lake Michigan, the docks seemed even busier than usual. Big ships made their way into port and dropped anchor in the Milwaukee River. Sirens and bells sounded warnings. Hurried dock workers shouted to each other in the rain.

No one noticed the skinny puppy wandering the docks. No one heard him when he barked nervously into the wind.

And no one saw where he ended up as the raindrops started to fall.

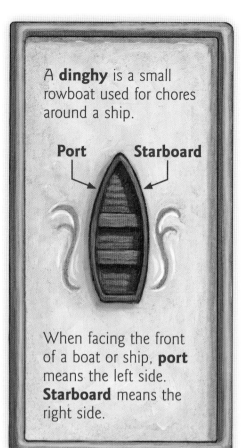

A **dinghy** is a small rowboat used for chores around a ship.

Port   Starboard

When facing the front of a boat or ship, **port** means the left side. **Starboard** means the right side.

Until the *Hyacinth* arrived.

"Off the starboard! Dog in the water! Dog in the water! Captain, we're taking the dinghy down."

Albert and Clifford didn't wait for their captain's okay. Quickly the two crewmen lowered the boat into the water. Albert and Clifford steered the dinghy, trying to reach the puppy before the river current carried him into the lake.

"Come here, pup! We'll help you," they called out over the wind. "Come on. We'll get you."

Just as they reached the dog, Albert reached out. He wrapped his hands around the puppy and pulled him to safety.

Back on the *Hyacinth*, some of the crew gathered around. Clifford toweled the puppy dry. "I can't believe it. The fur next to his body is dry. And he's not even shaking."

"Look at his paws," Albert said. "They're webbed like a duck!"

"What kind of dog is he?" Clifford wondered.

The captain ran his hands over the dog's head and down to his haunches. "He looks like he's part Newfoundland. A Newfie."

The captain knew that Newfies are great water dogs. Their double coat keeps them warm. And their webbed paws help them swim.

An idea formed in the captain's head.

"We could use a good ship dog. This dog could be the one."

Everyone liked this idea. They decided to name their new friend Sport. And that's how a homeless puppy found a home on a ship.

Sport had fun exploring his new home. He roamed from bow to stern, from port to starboard. He found places to sleep and stand watch, and especially to eat.

Three times a day, the cook rang a dinner bell. The crew hustled to the mess, where they found biscuits, stew, and fruit pies. Sport was a growing puppy. He was always the first to clean his plate.

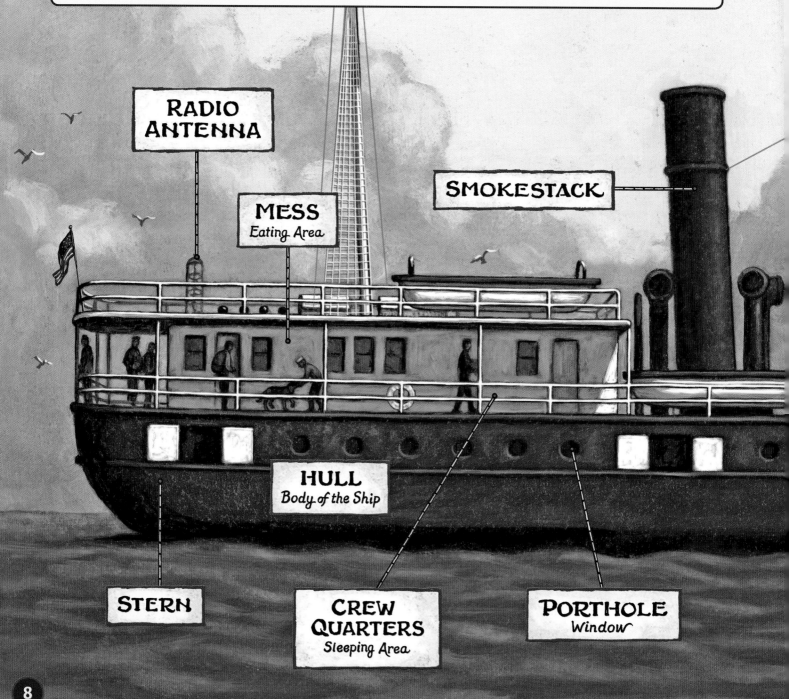

RADIO ANTENNA

MESS
Eating Area

SMOKESTACK

HULL
Body of the Ship

STERN

CREW QUARTERS
Sleeping Area

PORTHOLE
Window

In between meals, Sport watched the crew members as they worked. They loaded coal, kerosene, lamps, lumber, tools, paint, furniture, firewood, and even small boats onto the *Hyacinth*.

"Watch out for Sport," the crew members would call. Quickly, Sport learned to stay out of the way.

RADIO ROOM

MAST

JIB BOOM
Crane to lift Buoys

PILOTHOUSE
Steering Station

WELL DECK
Access to the Cargo Hold

BOW

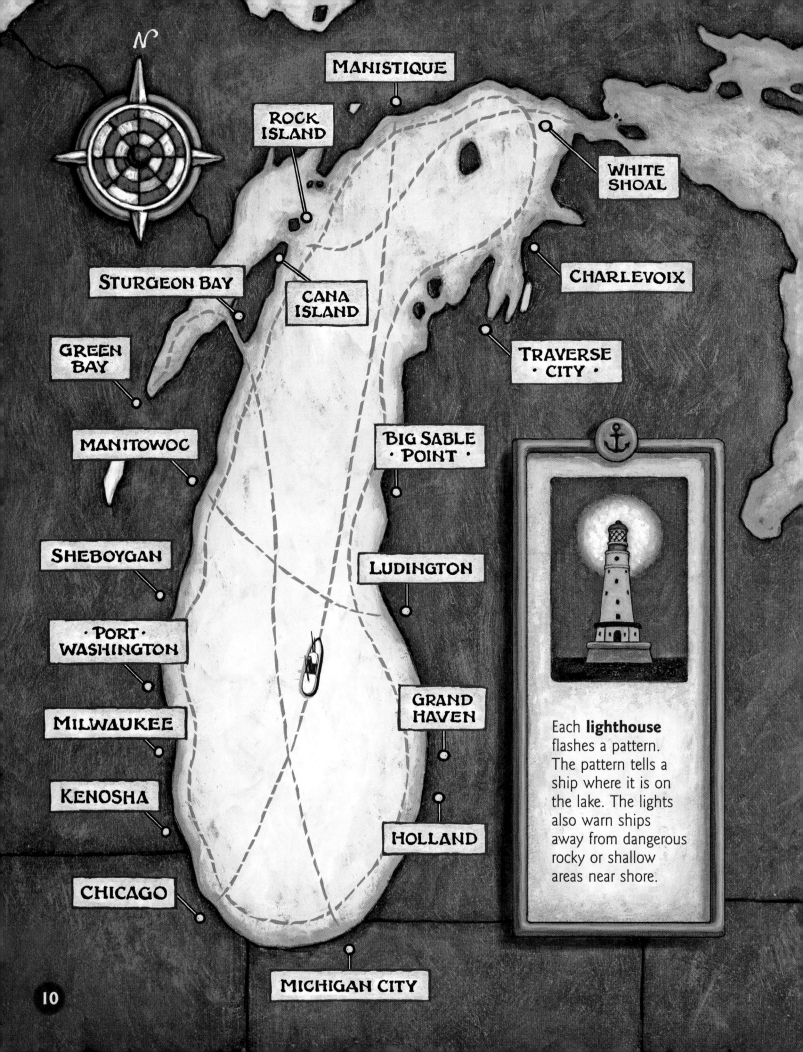

MANISTIQUE

ROCK ISLAND

WHITE SHOAL

STURGEON BAY

CANA ISLAND

CHARLEVOIX

GREEN BAY

TRAVERSE · CITY ·

MANITOWOC

BIG SABLE · POINT ·

SHEBOYGAN

LUDINGTON

· PORT · WASHINGTON

MILWAUKEE

GRAND HAVEN

KENOSHA

HOLLAND

CHICAGO

MICHIGAN CITY

Each **lighthouse** flashes a pattern. The pattern tells a ship where it is on the lake. The lights also warn ships away from dangerous rocky or shallow areas near shore.

The *Hyacinth* was a lighthouse tender. Its main job was to take supplies to the lighthouses on Lake Michigan. Soon Sport had friends all around the lake.

From rocky Manitowoc to sandy Ludington.

From windy Michigan City to calm Green Bay.

From busy Chicago to quiet Manistique.

Other ships blew their horns as they passed. They tooted a captain's salute—one long blast and two short blasts. This was a friendly way to say thank you for the work the *Hyacinth*'s crew did to keep other ships safe on the water.

Today the crew was preparing for another trip. Sport ran around deck looking in all the crates. The captain made sure the *Hyacinth* and its crew were ready.

"All cargo lashed and tight?"

"Aye, aye, captain!"

"Anchors pulled?"

"Aye, aye, captain!"

"Heave ho, we're off."

The engine shuddered as it powered up. Then the ship chugged away.

The *Hyacinth* steamed to the Cana Island Lighthouse.

The crew took supplies from the *Hyacinth* to Cana Island in a rowboat. When the rowboat got close to shore, the crew needed Sport's help.

"Okay, Sport," Albert said. "Show us how smart you are."

Albert shook out a rope and threw it into the water. Sport carried the line to shore. Then it could be used to pull the boat in.

The lighthouse keeper's family ran out to greet Sport. The children squealed in delight at the sight of a dog bringing them their supplies. When everything was unloaded, it was time to say goodbye. Sport and the *Hyacinth* crew had more stops to make.

"See you next time, Sport!" the children said.

Sport watched as the crew placed a buoy to mark a hidden shallow area near Big Sable Point Lighthouse.

Just as Clifford climbed to the top of the buoy to adjust the light, his tool bag dropped. Sport dove in. He grabbed the bag and dragged it back to the boat.

Albert steered the dinghy closer to the buoy so Clifford could climb aboard. Then they picked up Sport from the water.

"Let's get you home, Sport," Albert said. "We're not leaving you behind!"

The crew worked hard each spring. They had to get all the lights and buoys operating for the shipping and sailing season. The captain wanted his crew to have some fun too.

Often when the ship docked for the night, the crew would go ashore to play baseball. They played against crews from other ships.

One night, Sport ran onto the field to join his team. He wanted to play too! A player from the other team yelled, "Get that mutt off the field!"

But the crowd started yelling too. "Sport, Sport, Sport! We want Sport!"

And so Sport joined the team. He caught the ball and tagged players in the outfield. Of course, he needed someone else to bat for him!

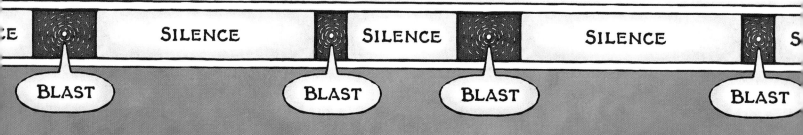

Foghorns help keep ships safe when it is too foggy to see. Each foghorn blasts in a different pattern.

CE | BLAST | SILENCE | BLAST | SILENCE | BLAST | SILENCE | BLAST | S

The patterns let ships know exactly where they are on the lake.

SILENCE — SILENCE — SILENCE — SIL

BLAST — BLAST — BLAST — BLAST

One morning the *Hyacinth* sailed into a thick fog. The quiet was eerie, unbroken by waves or wind. Then the sound of a horn broke the stillness.

It was the Grand Traverse Lighthouse's foghorn.

"Cut the engine, now!" the captain told his first officer. "Anchors down! Listen for any ships coming toward us."

Sport's ears twitched up. He ran to the bow, stopped, and let out an explosion of barks. Albert ran to Sport's side. He could just make out the outline of a passenger ship approaching. The other ship might not see the *Hyacinth* through the fog.

The captain grabbed the whistle cord and blew one long whistle, then two short whistles. He repeated the pattern twice. That signaled, "We're a stopped ship on open water!"

The two ships might have hit each other. But the crew on board the passenger ship heard the signal and pulled away just in time.

Sport liked when the *Hyacinth* visited Chicago. He always found new and exciting smells in the city. As the crew loaded coal, Sport often explored the docks. The captain would blow a whistle calling him back when it was time to leave. They had to leave on time. The lighthouse keepers around the lake were counting on them to make their deliveries.

One day, Sport wandered too far. A warehouse worker spotted him. He thought Sport looked like a good watchdog. He didn't know Sport already had a job.

The man looped a rope around Sport's neck and led him to a warehouse. Sport didn't know what was happening, or how he would get back to his ship.

The next day an ice wagon was out delivering ice to restaurants and grocery stores. The driver recognized Sport. He had seen him on the docks before.

"Sport, what are you doing here?" He turned to the warehouse worker. "This dog belongs on the *Hyacinth*. He needs to be returned to his ship!"

The iceman quickly untied the rope and told Sport to get in the wagon. "I'm getting you home, Sport!"

The ice wagon raced to the docks. Sport didn't see his ship or crew anywhere. The *Hyacinth* was gone. But he did see a ship he had seen before. The *Indiana* was one of the biggest ships on Lake Michigan.

"Is that Sport?" the captain of the *Indiana* called down. "If that's Sport, he can hitch a ride to Milwaukee with us!"

How lucky it was that so many people on the lake knew Sport.

Sport got to ride in the freight area of the *Indiana*. Soon children started coming down from the ship's dining room to meet him.

They all wanted to hear the stories of the ship dog

who fell into the Milwaukee River during a storm,

who joined a crew and lived on a ship,

who helped bring supplies to the lighthouses,

who played baseball,

who looked out for his crewmates on the *Hyacinth*,

and who had made friends all around the lake.

Afterward, the children told their families and friends about Sport.
And the story of Sport continued to spread.

Meeting the children on the passenger ship had been exciting. But Sport was happy to be back with his crew on the *Hyacinth*. He had good friends to play with tonight and important work to do tomorrow.

That night, Sport fell asleep to the sway of the ship and the sound of the water.

He was a ship dog, and this ship was his home.

THE REAL SPORT was believed to be a Newfoundland and retriever mix. This meant he was a friendly working dog and a good swimmer. He started life as a stray puppy on the docks of Milwaukee. No one knows how he ended up in the Milwaukee River one day. He might have fallen in. Or he might have been washed in during a rainstorm. *Hyacinth* crew members Albert Collins and Clifford Perry saw him in the water. They saved him from being carried into the lake. After his rescue, Sport lived on the *Hyacinth* from 1914 to 1926.

The *Hyacinth* was a lighthouse tender ship for the US Lighthouse Service and later the US Coast Guard. The word *tend* means to take care of something. The *Hyacinth* took care of the lighthouses, lightships, and buoys on Lake Michigan and Green Bay from 1903 to 1945.

Every spring, the crew set the buoys to mark places where ships needed to be careful. They placed lightships, special ships that act as lighthouses, in deep areas of the lake. For the rest of the shipping season, the *Hyacinth* crew maintained the buoys and lightships and made deliveries. It carried fuel and building supplies to the lighthouses, especially the ones offshore. A typical delivery included oil, coal, firewood, stone, and concrete. The ship even carried a library box with storybooks and learning materials. A visit from a ship dog like Sport was an extra treat for the lighthouse keepers and their families who lived away from the mainland.

Sport was a good friend to the crew members as they spent many months away from home. He even played on the crew's baseball team! But he also helped. He was good at fetching tools or chasing away pests. Sometimes the crew used a smaller boat to take supplies from the ship to a lighthouse. When they got close, Sport jumped out and swam to shore, carrying a line. Then someone on shore would use the line to pull the boat in. The other stories in this book are also based on jobs that Sport and the crew did every year to help keep the lake safe. A few are based on actual events, such as Sport getting lost and found in Chicago and then hitching a ride on the *Indiana*.

Sport died on July 19, 1926, of old age. He was given a sea burial off the coast of Ludington, Michigan. The crew gathered on deck in full uniform for the funeral. Sport was lowered into Lake Michigan as the crew saluted. After Sport died, *Hyacinth* Captain Harry Maynard wrote about him in the September 1, 1926, issue of *Lighthouse Service Bulletin*. "Sport was just a dog, but he was always a good dog and a good shipmate, a friend to everybody and everybody's friend," the captain wrote.

THE AUTHOR AND ILLUSTRATOR WOULD LIKE TO THANK the Milwaukee Public Museum for access to its archival materials on the *Hyacinth*. An MPM educator and photographer spent more than a month aboard the ship in 1926, toward the end of Sport's life, and the photographs and materials from this trip make the *Hyacinth* one of the most well-documented lighthouse tenders in US history. Access to these materials and the assistance of MPM curator Albert Muchka, who has researched the *Hyacinth* and its crew extensively, helped ensure the accuracy of historical details in the story and illustrations.

Published by the Wisconsin Historical Society Press
Publishers since 1855

The Wisconsin Historical Society helps people connect to the past by collecting, preserving, and sharing stories. Founded in 1846, the Society is one of the nation's finest historical institutions.
Join the Wisconsin Historical Society: wisconsinhistory.org/membership

Printed in the United States of America
Designed by Shawn Biner

23 22 21   3 4 5

Library of Congress Cataloging-in-Publication Data
Names: Cameron, Pamela, author. | Graef, Renée, illustrator.
Title: Sport : ship dog of the Great Lakes / written by Pamela Cameron ; Illustrated by Renée Graef.
Description: [Madison, WI] : Wisconsin Historical Society Press, [2019] | Audience: Ages 0–9. | Audience: Grade K–3. |
Identifiers: LCCN 2018038999 (print) | LCCN 2018049532 (ebook) | ISBN 9780870209154 | ISBN 9780870209147 (casebound : alk. paper) | ISBN 9780870209154 (ebk.)
Subjects: LCSH: Lighthouse tenders—Great Lakes Region (North America)—Juvenile literature. | Lighthouse keepers—Michigan, Lake—History—Juvenile literature. | Working dogs—Great Lakes Region (North America)—Juvenile literature.
Classification: LCC VK1023.3 (ebook) | LCC VK1023.3 .C36 2019 (print) | DDC 386/.85509774—dc23
LC record available at https://lccn.loc.gov/2018038999